The BEST of
BUDDY the
Bluenose
Reindeer

The BEST of BUDDY the Bluenose Reindeer

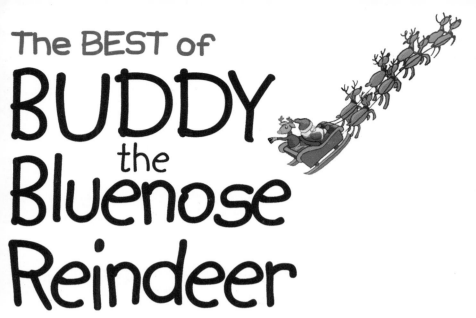

BRUCE NUNN
Illustrations by
Brenda Jones

NIMBUS
PUBLISHING

Nimbus Publishing Limited
PO Box 9166
Halifax, NS   B3K 5M8
(902) 455-4286

Printed and bound in Canada

Library and Archives Canada Cataloguing in Publication

    Nunn, Bruce, 1962-
    The best of Buddy the bluenose reindeer / Bruce
    Nunn ; illustrations by Brenda Jones.

    ISBN 978-1-55109-871-5

I. Jones, Brenda, 1953- II. Title.

PS8577.U5485B48 2011   jC813'.6   C2011-903922-2

Nimbus Publishing acknowledges the financial support for its publishing
activities from the Government of Canada through the Canada Book
Fund (CBF) and the Canada Council for the Arts, and from the Province
of Nova Scotia through the Department of Communities, Culture and
Heritage.

For all Nova Scotians,
at home and away.

Buddy the Bluenose Reindeer

ou know Santa's eight
reindeer, don't you? Let's
see...there are Dasher
and Dancer, of course.
And Prancer and Vixen...Oh!
And who can forget Comet and
Cupid and Donner—although
some say "Donder"—and...
ummmm...oh, yeah: Blitzen.

Everybody knows those names. And then of course there is reindeer number nine, Santa's most famous reindeer of all: Rudolph.

But we never hear about reindeer number ten. He was added to Santa's team of sleigh-pullers a long time ago, but he doesn't usually fly with the others. You see, reindeer number ten is an extra. He's a reindeer replacement. A backup buck, you might say.

Now, I'm not talking about Olive. This isn't "Olive, the other reindeer." That's just the kids' joke about the song. No, this special reindeer is a little four-legged fellow who grew up in the woods on the South Shore of Nova Scotia. Just wait till you hear. This Nova Scotian reindeer can ALSO guide Santa's sleigh at night because he too has a brightly illuminated proboscis!

What does that mean? Let's just say he HAS A VERY SHINY NOSE.

And, as a matter of fact, if you ever
saw it, YOU would even say it glows.
It shines a brilliant, beautiful hue. It's
true. This reindeer is uniquely Nova
Scotian. You see, we've all heard about
Rudolph, the Red-nosed Reindeer,
but this little fellow is BUDDY, the
BLUENOSE REINDEER!

Now, even though Buddy is a
reindeer and his nose is an unusual
colour, he's altogether different from
Rudolph. But he is related.
Buddy is Rudolph's first
cousin, once removed,
on his mother's
side. A typical
Nova Scotian
family connection.
Though, if you
asked me the
classic Nova Scotian
question, "What's
his father's name?"…I'm
not sure I could answer.
I think it's Angus.

Anyway, Buddy the Bluenose Reindeer joined Santa's famous gang up at the North Pole. Now, I know what you're thinking. You're guessing that all of the other reindeer used to laugh and call him names. Am I right?

Nahhh! The other reindeer were fine with Buddy's blue schnozz. After all, they were used to differences in appearance, what with Rudolph's remarkable redness and all. They didn't judge. They liked Buddy and his nose and the story of his Nova Scotian past.

But I'm getting ahead of myself. Here's how Buddy came to join their team:

It was the eve of Christmas Eve, the day before the day before Christmas, to be exact, and Santa was getting frantic.

His guiding light, the trusty Rudolph, wasn't feeling well. He was sneezing and wheezing and sniffling and whiffling.

"Oh no!" thought Santa. Rudolph had a cold in his red nose. And it was a bad one, too. This was a Christmas crisis: Rudolph was going to be too under the weather to fly over the weather. With Christmas quickly approaching, how could Santa fly without his bright light to guide him through the sky?

Meanwhile, blue-nosed Buddy,
down in Nova Scotia, was having some
problems of his own. You see, this all
happened years ago, back in the age of
wooden sailing ships, and Buddy had
been adopted as a mascot on board a
Nova Scotian fishing schooner.

They say this little deer was from
Port Joli, which makes sense. But he
was having a very unjolly time fitting
in. Oh sure, the captain liked him.

Captain Nick was his name. Nick
Klaus. From Lunenburg, he was.
His wife, Clara Klaus, came from
Christmas Island, Cape Breton. She
was on board too and she really took a
shining to Buddy's nose, so to speak.

The crew, however…well, that was
another story. They were a bit jealous.

They didn't want Buddy on their ship. In fact, THEY used to laugh and call him names. And they never let poor Buddy play in their FUN DORY GAMES.

Out at sea, you see, the fishermen used to have a great time. They would jump in their wooden rowboats—called dories—and get lowered down the side of the ship. Once they were down, they would row out to their nets as fast as they could. It was a race! It was wonderful fun.

But Buddy, sweet Buddy, the Bluenose reindeer, wasn't allowed to

12

play. Those crabby fishermen wouldn't let Buddy in a boat. Wouldn't allow him to get lowered down, to play in the rowing games. It was very sad.

Buddy was sorry he had no dory. The poor little deer was feeling rather...blue. As you might expect.

But, that all changed on this legendary eve of Christmas Eve. Well, actually it was a foggy, choppy, salt-sprayin', blowin'-a-gale, hurricane-force eve of Christmas Eve! Thecaptain hadn't planned to be on the seas in such rough weather, but a nasty winter squall had roared up so fast that the ship and crew were caught unaware and unprepared.

The schooner lurched wildly on the waves, and the normally tough crew was starting to look scared. Under black clouds, the schooner was at risk of smashing against rocks hidden by the growing darkness of the storm. Captain Nick grabbed the wheel tighter and, squinting against the driving drizzle, he desperately tried to steer his ship blindly

through the storm. But it was hopeless.
He could barely see.

Just then he caught sight of Buddy
up by the mainmast, straining with the
rest of the crew on the ropes. As Buddy
looked back, he saw the captain carefully
walking up the slippery wooden deck.

On that drizzly, foggy eve of
Christmas Eve, the captain came to say:

"Buddy, with your nose so blue…
won't you guide our schooner
through?"

Sure enough, Buddy stepped forward on the slick, slanted deck. Rearing up, he fixed himself proudly in place at the bow of the bobbing schooner. He stuck his bright blue nose out over the bowsprit and lighted the schooner's way through the darkness, past the dangerous rocky shores where the waves were crashing.

Buddy stayed at his post until the vessel was guided right through the Atlantic storm and into calm waters. He saved the ship! And the crew too! Buddy came through the crisis with flying colours.

(And, just as an aside, THAT is why Nova Scotia's famous schooner is known to this day as "Bluenose"...because of that dear little deer, not afraid to stick his nose out when needed.)

Captain Nick and Clara Klaus
were thrilled and relieved that the ship
was rescued. The captain decided to
reward Buddy with a big surprise. He
would let the little deer join him in the
captain's very own rowboat: Buddy
was going to be lowered down to join
in the fishermen's rowing races. Then,
how the schooner crew loved him!

And they shouted out with glee! They
pointed to the captain and shouted:
 "Buddy the Bluenose Reindeer...
YOU'LL GO DOWN IN
HIS DOR-Y!"

Everyone on board cheered and clapped and celebrated.

Now, guess who was watching over this festive scene? It was that jolly old fellow who sees you when you're sleeping and knows when you're awake: Santa Claus! Santa was smiling because he knew that Buddy had been a good deer, good, for goodness' sake. And he saw the solution to his own nosey problem.

"Why, that little deer is a Rudolph of another colour," Santa chuckled to himself. Later that night, just after finishing his last-minute Christmas preparations, Santa swooped down to Nova Scotia in his magical sleigh. He was going to make Buddy an offer he couldn't refuse. He wanted Buddy to become his best back-up reindeer: Rudolph's stand-in. Santa asked Buddy if he would be a replacement bulb to shine the way for his quickly approaching Christmas eve flight. Buddy was overjoyed at the invitation! Filling in for the famous Rudolph? That's a reindeer's dream come true. He would be thrilled to lend his nose to Santa's cause.

So, with Captain Nick, Clara Klaus, and the schoonermen all waving and wishing him luck, the Bluenose reindeer flew off with Santa in his sleigh, headed for the North Pole. Considering all that had happened, Buddy was glad for his blue nose. He couldn't wait to join Santa's team of reindeer.

But…he was just a little worried. He could sail and he could row, but he was pretty sure that he didn't know how to fly. How exactly, he wondered to himself, was a simple schooner deer from

Nova Scotia going to take to the air with a team of magical flying reindeer on Christmas Eve? Buddy was puzzling that problem as the sleigh swooped down and slid to a stop.

Santa's workshop was busy, busy, busy. The elves were frantic with last-minute toy tinkering, and the other reindeer were carefully checking their harnesses for any last-minute fixes.

For the first time, Buddy could see the
other deer up close, all eight of them:
Dasher and Dancer and Prancer
and Vixen, Comet and Cupid, and
Donner and Blitzen. About as big
as a schooner crew, thought Buddy.
And that made Santa their skipper.
Captain Christmas!

Just then, Rudolph himself stepped
forward. Buddy was nervous. What
would Rudolph think of having a
replacement deer of a different colour?
Would his nose be out of joint?
Rudolph sneezed. Then he snorted in
the cold air and drew closer. The two
deer came nose to nose, and Rudolph's
red glow looked sickly and sore. Buddy's
snout was shiny like a bright blue bulb
on a Christmas tree. As the two bucks

shared their two cents' worth their noses formed a purplish halo of light.

"How's she goin', cousin?" said Rudolph. "What's goin' on?"

Buddy smiled a big smile. Rudolph was glad to see him. The two distant deer cousins laughed and got caught up on news from back home. He told Rudolph about his schooner adventures back in Nova Scotia, and Rudolph told Buddy exciting stories of pulling Santa's sleigh in Christmases past. The two shiny-nosed deer were brightly lighted and delighted.

The next day was the big day. It was a foggy Christmas Eve. And Santa came to say, "Rudolph with your nose so red, you better take an Aspirin and go to bed!"

Then Santa turned to say, "Buddy, with your nose so blue…"

"Yes, yes," said Buddy, "I'd LOVE to!"

His chance to light Santa's sleigh in Rudolph's place had finally come! The reindeer crew couldn't believe it. They wondered if young Buddy was really ready for such a big job. After all, how could they complete Santa's traditional Christmas Eve gift-giving journey

around the world with a rookie, substitute deer lighting the way? They just didn't think the idea would fly. And they knew for sure that Buddy couldn't. How would this work?

Buddy was certainly beginning to wonder what Santa had in mind.

The big magical red bag of presents was prepared. The long, long list was checked and checked again. Santa's red suit was pressed and ready. Then it was time to bring toys and joys to good girls and boys all over the world.

With a wink and whistle, Santa
Claus called to Buddy and the other
reindeer. He led them through the
snow, out behind his workshop.

"But…but…the sleigh is out front,"
said Buddy, feeling confused.

As Buddy and his buddies rounded the corner, they looked up in amazement. They couldn't believe what their eyes were seeing. Santa Claus, with his big red bag of toys, was standing high up on the deck of a huge wooden fishing schooner.

"I borrowed this from my good friends Nick and Clara Klaus down in Nova Scotia," said Santa with a twinkle in his eye.

Something magical had happened to the ship—it was floating in the air, above the snow! And of course it had been painted a bright Christmas red. Thousands of tiny, sparkling lights flashed like fireflies all around the vessel. It was awesome!

"Ho, ho, heeeeave ho!" shouted
Santa, pointing down to the ropes
that kept the magic floating vessel anchored to land. The reindeer
jumped to it. All hooves on deck!
They untied the schooner, and pulled
up the ropes. They each wiggled into
the sleigh harnesses that had been
lashed to the bow of the schooner.
And with that, Santa's reindeer leaped
for the sky. There was a powerful

"whoosh" sound as they lifted the big ship up, up into the air. Anchors aweigh! The good ship *Christmas* sailed into the night with Santa at the helm. Up at the bow of the strange flying ship stood Buddy the Bluenose Reindeer. Like an oddly coloured lighthouse, the bright blue beacon on his snout lit up the darkness. The flying reindeer in front pulled the big schooner faster and faster through the starry sky. Swooshing down to rooftops, Santa went "ashore" from his sailing ship to deliver his Christmas cargo down the chimneys. He had gifts for all the kids of the right toy age for the voyage.

For Buddy, this trip was more fun than any dory race! All too soon, though, the night was nearly over. Santa had just one more house to visit.

Way out in the ocean is the Nova
Scotian island called Sable, which is just
a thin strip of land. Buddy knew it from
his sailing days. Only one family lived
on Sable Island, in a small house. Wild
horses ran by in herds, over snow-
covered sand dunes. The children
hoped and wished that Santa would

find them way out there. They weren't wishing for a pony that Christmas; they already had plenty. They were hoping for shiny new toys that made lots of noise. And new storybooks too. And candy.

Now, hang on to your hat. This is where the story gets even more exciting.

Santa's flying schooner swooped down toward the narrow little island. As the open sea came closer, Buddy could see from his perch at the bow

that a winter storm was swirling
below. Not again! he thought. But
this one was worse than any ocean
storm the sailor deer had ever seen.
Giant crashing waves smashed onto
the island's snowy beaches. The wind
blew in great blustery gusts. The
reindeer strained to keep their magic
flying ship upright. It was not a good
scene at all.

Onward the flying reindeer flew! Dashing through the snow, they set one course all the way. But the roof of the island house was icy, and the zooming schooner was moving too fast. In the blink of an eye, it skipped off the house and landed with a splash out in the stormy ocean waves.

The freezing winter air made thick
ice form quickly all over the schooner. The ship was too heavy now for
the reindeer to lift. Strong winds were
pushing the schooner sideways toward
the island's shore. They were going to
be shipwrecked on the beach!

Buddy had enough sailor sense to
know that something had to be done
right away. Santa wasn't used to sailing

a ship that couldn't fly, especially on a
dark and stormy night. Buddy
signalled the other reindeer to heave
on the ropes. Up went the big white
sails and they filled with wind in an
instant.

The red schooner zoomed across
the choppy water, heading straight for
the shoreline. In the bright blue light

from Buddy's shiny nose, Santa could see the sand bar coming at them.

"Ho ho hooold on!" he called out, grasping tight to the ship's wheel. The reindeer braced themselves. Under full sail, at top speed, that Christmas schooner plowed head-on into the sandy strip of shore. With a great shudder, the ship pushed its way through to the open water on the other side.

They made it! Buddy saved the ship! The deer all cheered. Santa cheered too.

Phhhhew! That was close. When
it comes to sailing in times of trouble,
Buddy "nose" what to do.

Oh, and don't worry about the
island kids. As the ship cut across that
sandbar, Santa tossed their toys ashore
in a big wooden captain's trunk. What
a wonderful Christmas treasure they
found in the sand when they woke up
the next morning. X-mas marks the
spot!

The ice melted away from the schooner, and with a "Ho ho hoooome!" Santa signalled his reindeer to fly.

Schwoosh!…the red schooner *Christmas* swept high into the night sky once again. It was headed on a course due north.

BUDDY

And this time, Buddy the Bluenose
Reindeer would go down in HISTOR–Y.

❅ ❅ ❅

At least, that's the way I heard it.

It's a story Santa loved to tell, of a
very Merry Christmas…

and a
Happy New Deer!

Buddy the Bluenose Reindeer

Reindeer

and the

Boston Christmas
Tree Adventure

ou know that wonderful old story called *The Night Before Christmas*, don't you? Sure. It's the one about Saint Nicholas. You know, with the round belly that shook when he laughed, like a bowl full of jelly. Remember? The one about the visions of sugar plums dancing in your head. Yeah, that's the one. Jelly bellies and sugar-plum heads. Who could ever forget that story?

Well, this Christmas story is exactly different from that one. And it's also quite differently the same. It's about a very special Christmas tree in Nova Scotia, and the little four-legged fellow who became part of that tree's big adventure.

Are you ready? Here's how it goes:

'Twas the night before Christmas, when all through the…

No, wait a minute. 'Twasn't the night before. 'Twas about…um…twenty-four nights before. Yeah, that's right.

'Twas twenty-four nights before Christmas, and all through Nova Scotia, not a creature was stirring except…

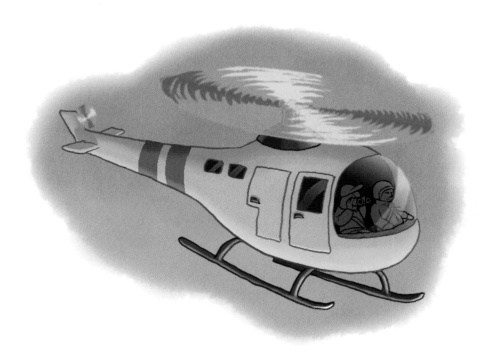

Zzzzooooooooooooom! A HELICOPTER!

It zipped along the tips of the snow-covered trees like Santa's sleigh over the rooftops.

The helicopter was on a hunt. A Christmas tree hunt. Pilot Pete and his pal were searching, searching, searching. Government workers, they were. Flying in duplicate. That means two of them: the pilot, Pete, and his lookout, Lou. They were Christmas tree experts on a Christmas tree mission.

They were looking for the tallest, roundest, greenest, cleanest, bestest, most awesome Christmas tree in all of Nova Scotia!

In other words, it had to be right some good. In fact, it had to be right some *perfect*.

"Precisely shaped, nicely green, branches well-spaced, no gaps between" was their boss's order. Oh yeah, that and "Tall. Really, really tall."

They had to find a big tree. Big enough to be Nova Scotia's Christmas present to a whole city, far away.

Their Christmas tree hunt was taking days and days. They zipped and they zoomed all over the place in their busy helicopter. They searched, they stared, they judged and compared. Like two Christmas shoppers in a big Christmas chopper. But so far, no luck.

They just could not find the exactly right
one. And they were running out of time.

Oh, they saw a lot of trees. But not THE
tree, you see? Where could it be? They had
looked almost EVERYWHERE.

The pilot in his helmet,
his pal in her cap,
had flown all over
the Nova Scotia map.

The perfect tall tree seemed to be just unfindable! Pete and his pal wondered and worried. They even wrote a little poem about their problem:

"Over Tatamagouche, Antigonish,
    and Ingonish too;
From Yarmouth to Canso and on
    to Mabou.
From Cape Breton to Cape Sable,
    we flew by the shore.
We tried Wedgeport, Lockport,
    Freeport and more.
The Annapolis Valley, Windsor to
    Bear River.
We tried Parrsboro and Amherst,
    but we still can't deliver!
We must find that perfect tree.
Wherever it may be!"

The tree had to be tall, but time was getting short. Darkness was falling. And this was Pete and Lou's last day of tree hunting. They had to choose a tree so they could get it to the faraway city in time. Everyone there was waiting, planning a city-sized Christmas tree party. The pilot and his pal knew it had to be now, they just didn't know how!

Then, a bright glow in the white snow caught the lookout's eye.

"Wait a second, what's that?" said Lookout Lou to Pilot Pete. "You have to circle back, fast."

Pilot Pete agreed.

A wink of his eye, and a twist of his head,
let his partner know she had nothing to dread.
He spoke not a word but went straight to work.
The chopper slowed down, and turned with a jerk.

They circled over a snow-covered
clearing. An old farmhouse sat on the hill. A
magnificent spruce tree stood like a statue in
the open field.

The tree was very, very tall. It bristled with
bushy boughs. The grandest evergreen ever
seen! And it was glowing from within.

A colourful light shone up through the tree's spreading branches. Someone was sending a signal to the pilot in the sky. Lou noticed right away. A big green tree glowing in the white snow is hard to miss.

"It looks like it's already lit up for Christmas," said Lookout Lou to Pilot Pete. They were amazed.

There on the crest of the new-fallen snow, beneath the green tree, was a bright blue glow!

Then the blue light started to move out from under the tree's big bottom branches. The two helicopter flyers were surprised.

When what to their wondering
eyes should appear,
But a fine four-legged fellow
—a Nova Scotia reindeer!

The deer was different from most. His snout was brightly lighted like a brilliant Christmas bulb.

"Hey, he has a very shiny nose," said Pilot Pete.

Santa's most famous reindeer of all? Nope. Close, but not quite. This little dude had a schnozz of a very different shade.

That little old pilot
with his helicopter buzzin'…
he knew in a moment
it was Rudolph's first cousin.

The bright blue light on the little deer's face was a clear clue. A blue clue. This wasn't Rudolph, the Red-nosed Reindeer.

No, this little guy was uniquely Nova Scotian. "Why, that's Buddy, the Bluenose Reindeer!"

Pilot Pete was right. Buddy was a dear little deer who grew up in the woods of Nova Scotia. A Bluenose reindeer through and through, he was. Once, he even sailed on a fishing schooner in a storm and rescued the ship with his shiny blue nose! (That was the year Santa Claus needed Buddy to fill in for Rudolph, who was sick on Christmas Eve. But that's another story.)

Lookout Lou wondered out loud: "How did that little reindeer down there know we were looking for a tree just like that one?"

"Maybe Christmas magic," said Pete. It was just a guess.

Actually, Buddy had read all about their Christmas tree hunt in the *Reindeer Report*, Santa's special newsletter for his reindeer team; a reindeer flyer for reindeer flyers.

Finding one specific tree in all the forests of Nova Scotia would be like finding a snowball

in a snowstorm. But Buddy read these instructions from Santa Claus himself:

Follow your nose to a place in the woods where a farmhouse sits on a hill. Twins live there, a boy and a girl. Their Christmas excitement is growing as big and beautiful as the tree outside their window.

You will know it when you see it.

The notice was signed at the bottom in large looping letters: "Yours truly, Buddy's buddy—Santa."

That's how Buddy found himself under the perfect tree. But Buddy knew Pilot Pete couldn't see the tree for the forest. That's when he had his bright idea. A bright blue idea!

You see, Buddy's blue nose glows even when it snows. His shiny nose marked the spot of the perfect tree treasure. That's when the helicopter flyers saw the light and swooped down.

The evening darkness was growing darker. Snowflakes fell like feathers. Buddy stood by the tree, beaming with pride.

His eyes, how they twinkled!
His dimples, how merry!
His cheeks were like roses,
his nose, a blueberry!
His droll little mouth
was drawn up like a bow.
He signalled with his nose
so Pete would know where to go.

His shiny snout guided the helicopter through the darkness like a lighthouse showing a lost ship the shore.

Pilot Pete pointed,
and to his pal,
gave a whistle.
And down they both flew,
like the down of a thistle.

(Perhaps a purple Nova Scotia thistle.)

Their helicopter floated over the roof of
the farmhouse.

Their chopper, it hung
by the chimney with care
in hopes that the big tree
soon would be theirs.

Inside the house, a family was sleeping. Or trying to.

The farm children were nestled
all snug in their beds.
While visions of helicopters
danced in their heads.

CHOPPA
    CHOPPA
        CHOPPA
            CHOPPA
                CHOPPA—

"Hey, that's not a vision," said young Rory to Frances.

Up, over the house
there arose such a clatter
He jumped up and ran
to see what was going on.

Or, you might say...

he sprang from his bed
to see what was the matter.

Yeah, that's better. Young Rory was so excited—

Away to the window
he flew like a flash.
He looked up and shuddered
and knocked over the trash.

Oops.

"It really is a helicopter! Wake up! Wake up!" Rory called to Frances.

The blue light on the crest of
the new-fallen snow
made a perfect landing spot
for the chopper to go.
So away from the house top,
Pilot Pete flew,
and landed next to the tree
in a halo of blue.

The pilot and his pal climbed out to say hi.
"How's she goin', Buddy?" said Pete.
"Merry Christmas," said Lou.
Before Buddy could finish greeting his flyer
friends, he was surprised by a noise.

The family—young Rory and Frances, and their mom and dad—were running toward the tree, all bundled in winter wear. And bouncing behind, Sable the dog and the two kittens too: Jigs and Reels.

The twins couldn't believe what they were seeing. There was a helicopter in their field. And a reindeer too! And his nose was blue! And their favourite tall tree was all lit up with his blue shine.

"It's awesome," said Pete to Lou. "The tallest one we've ever found."

"Way to go, Buddy," they said with relief. "We are delighted that you are so lighted. We would never have seen this great tree if you weren't so nosey, so to speak. It's perfect. How did you know we needed a tree just like this?"

Buddy just grinned his little Buddy grin.

Pete turned to the twins and said, "Congratulations, your tall tree is just what we were looking for. Can we use it as the Boston Tree?"

"The Boston Tree?" asked Frances with a giggle.

Rory was confused too. "I know about spruce trees, maple trees, and apple trees. But what's a Boston Tree?" he asked.

The twins' mom and dad smiled. Pilot Pete smiled too.

"It's not a *kind* of tree," said Pete. "It's a place for the tree to be."

He explained that every year a tree is chosen to be Nova Scotia's Christmas present to the big city of Boston.

"It's a short trip away by ship," said Pete. "Down in a place we used to call the Boston States.

"The Boston people will put up your tree in the middle of their big city. They'll decorate it with lights. Thousands of people will come out to see your tree light up. There'll be fireworks and music and dancing. There'll be cheering and clapping and singing. And maybe fiddles.

"The mayor will give a speech about your
tree. And it will all be on TV for people all
over the world to see, at Christmastime.

"Your tree will be famous. Everyone loves the Boston Tree. Each year we pick the best one we can find. Buddy's discovery is the best yet. We couldn't have found it without him."

"Cool!" said both kids at the same time.

"You can definitely use our tree as the Boston Tree," said Frances. "But why does Boston get a tree?"

Pilot Pete bent down to answer the question. "There's an important story to tell about that," he said.

Buddy pawed the snow with his hoof. He pricked up his ears to listen closely. "Almost a hundred years ago," Pete began, "there was a big blast in Nova Scotia's capital city."

He told them about the two ships in Halifax Harbour. About the way they crashed close to shore. About the big boom they caused. It blew down houses and buildings.

"It happened at this time of year," Pete explained. "Just before Christmas. Part of the city was a wreck.

"People needed help. Especially when it snowed the next day.

That's when people packed their bags in Boston and came up to Nova Scotia to lend a

hand. A whole trainful came. Just like friendly neighbours, they wanted to help. They brought gifts, too. Things people in Halifax needed, like blankets and medicine.

"They sent us a train so we send them a tree every year," said Pete.

"It's the Boston Christmas Tree. It's a giant Christmas present to say thanks."

Rory and Frances were more thrilled than ever. They couldn't wait to see the exciting tree lighting. A Boston Tree party!

But first, this big present had to be wrapped and delivered. There wasn't much time to spare.

The next day, a team of tree experts came to the house in the field. They brought a big crane and a tree cradle. And a long, flat truck, too. The tree team swarmed the tall tree like Santa's busy elves.

Buddy the Bluenose Reindeer nosed his way in to check the work.

They bundled the branches carefully and tied them tight. That was so the boughs wouldn't break when down came the Christmas tree, needles and all.

Next, they wrapped the whole tree with a great big wrapper. They even tied it with a bow made of rope.

Then the chainsaw's busy buzz filled the air. Buzzzzzzzzzzzzzzzzzzzzzzzzzz!

The tall, wrapped gift tree was gently lowered onto the big flat truck.

Everyone cheered and clapped and celebrated. Rory and Frances made a sign to put on the tree. It said, "To Boston: Merry Christmas and thanks from Nova Scotia."

The tree was tied down. The truck engine roared. It was time to go. But Pilot Pete looked at his watch, and he also looked worried.

"This tree has a long way to go and short time to get there," said Pete. "We need to make sure our gift isn't late."

Then Pete turned to say, "Buddy, with your nose so blue, won't you guide our big tree through?"

Hmmm…Buddy thought he had heard something like that before.

"Sure," said Buddy. "I'd be happy to."

So up to the truck top,
Buddy he flew,
with a heart full of hope
and good wishes, too.
And then in a twinkling,
they heard on the truck,
The prancing and pawing
of a small reindeer buck.

Buddy sat on top of the bundled-up tree.
"Let's go!" he called.

His colourful nose lit up the night like a
police car light on top of the moving truck.

More rapid than eagles,
of course that truck flew.
The driver whistled and shouted
and sang Christmas songs too.

"Oh Christmas tree, Oh Christmas tree! I love your speeeeding branches!"

The tree truck rumbled down the road. Cars pulled to the side to make room for the blue-lighted tree bound for Boston. Spruce needles fluttered in the air.

With that little old driver,
so lively and quick,
Buddy knew in a moment
it would be a fast trip.

A ship loaded with big boxy containers was waiting at the harbour wharf. A crane hook came down from the sky. It lifted the long tree off the back of the truck. Buddy held on tight.

Laying his hoof alongside
his blue nose,
and giving a nod,
UP to the ship he rose.

The little deer looked down at the harbour. It was the place that once had that big blast in the past. Buddy thought about that for a moment.

Some snowflakes started to flutter.

Time to set sail now. The blue-nosed reindeer signalled the captain, who ordered all his Nova Scotia sailors into action.

He whistled, and shouted,
and called them by name;
"Now, Dauphinee!
Now Doucette!
Now Purdy and Visser!
On Corkum!
On Capstick!
On Donald and Zwicker!

From the top of his perch,
Buddy heard the loud call.
"Now, heave away,
haul away, heave away all!"

The crew dashed away to untie the big ship. The captain shouted his orders. Captain Nick was his name. Nick Klaus. From Lunenburg, he was. He was named after his grandfather, who sailed on the *Bluenose* fishing schooner in the old days. Nick's grandmother, Clara, did too. Buddy once sailed with them on a Christmas voyage. But that's another story.

Captain Nick waved to Buddy from his wheelhouse, where he would steer the ship. He knew how important this tree delivery would be.

At first, the ocean voyage was fine and fun. Then, the waves got huge. The wind blew hard. The sky opened up. Wet snow fell fast. Everything got blustery, gustery, nasty and dark. Stormy seas tried to swallow the big ship, Christmas tree and all!

The huge metal ship plowed up one side of each giant wave, and down the other. Wave after wave, again and again. Buddy the Bluenose Reindeer managed to keep his place on top of the tree. He squinted into the slanted snow.

There was a sound somewhere in the darkness. A horn! Out in the black night, a fishing boat was getting too close. The two ships were not going to pass in the night. They were going to crash!

Captain Nick couldn't see the small boat in the snowy blackness. He sounded his ship's deep booming horn as a warning. But the night was too dark and stormy—no one could see.

The tree ship was going to hit the fish boat! Holy mackerel, this could be a disaster!

The captain called up to Buddy for help. "Buddy! I blew the ship's horn. I blew and I blew. Now I need you to use your blue too!"

Buddy knew just what the captain meant. He stood up tall in the stiff wind. He held tight to the tree as best he could. He stuck his brilliant blue nose into the dark sky. His shiny blue beam scanned the sea like a searchlight.

It worked. The captain caught sight of
something in the light. Dead ahead! A fishing
boat, right there! His big ship was almost on
top of it. Captain Nick grabbed the ship's
controls. He steered his ship sharply to the
right. Just in time! The two boats barely
missed each other. Both sailed away safely.

"Pheeew. That was close," said Captain Nick.

Buddy saved the ship! And the Boston Tree, too! The sailors all cheered and threw their caps in the air.

When it comes to sailing in times of trouble, Buddy still "nose" what to do. Cousin Rudolph would be proud. I think Santa would be too.

BUDDY

In the morning, the ship docked safely at Boston Harbour. A great crane lifted the precious Christmas cargo onto another long truck. A police car led the tree truck into the city, all the way to a wide-open city park called the Boston Common. The park was all spruced up to put the spruce up.

The tree was unwrapped and decorated with many lights. But they were not turned on. Not yet. The big tree-lighting party would happen soon.

Nighttime came. And people too.
Thousands and thousands of people circled
around the Nova Scotia tree. The crowd
waited in the cool air for the special moment
to come: the exciting lighting!

On a big stage, a Christmas ceilidh (say it "kay-lee") was in full swing. Singers sang and dancers danced. Children laughed and giggled. Cameras flashed. And speechmakers made speeches:

"Ladies and Gentlemen…this tree is a gift for a very special reason. The little sign on the side says it all: 'To Boston: Merry Christmas and thanks from Nova Scotia.'"

Then the fiddle music started again.

The music grew louder. The crowd grew crowder. The city was watching and waiting. The Christmas tree lighting in Boston was about to happen. People back home in Nova Scotia watched their TVs to see the Boston Tree come to life.

Everyone wondered who was going to be the special guest tree lighter, the one who would push the big black switch to light up the tree for all to see.

A white spotlight hit the stage. Out walked Rory and Frances and their whole family from back home. Even Jigs and Reels were there. And Sable too, bouncing and barking!

And, in the middle, their new friend, Buddy.

Buddy looked up at the tree, smiled, and stepped forward. With his bulbous blue nose, the Nova Scotia reindeer pushed the big light switch to light the tree lights.

"Oooooh!" the crowd said. "Ahhhhhh!" they said next.

Gazillions of colourful Christmas lights burst into full glow, a reindeer rainbow! The lights danced and sparkled in the children's wide eyes. It was awesome. The clapping and cheering didn't stop for a long, long time. The Christmas tree party went on late into the night.

The crowd was still singing Christmas carols when the big truck started to drive away. And guess who was on it? Standing on the back, where the Boston Tree used to be, was Buddy the Bluenose Reindeer. He was heading back home.

But I heard him exclaim,
as he drove out of sight,
"Happy Christmas to all,
and to all a good night!"

The Night Before Christmas
(originally published in 1823 under the title
"A Visit from St. Nicholas")

by Clement Clark Moore

'Twas the night before Christmas, when all through the house
Not a creature was stirring, not even a mouse;
The stockings were hung by the chimney with care,
In hopes that St. Nicholas soon would be there;
The children were nestled all snug in their beds,
While visions of sugar-plums danced in their heads;
And mamma in her 'kerchief, and I in my cap,
Had just settled our brains for a long winter's nap,
When out on the lawn there arose such a clatter,
I sprang from the bed to see what was the matter.
Away to the window I flew like a flash,
Tore open the shutters and threw up the sash.
The moon on the breast of the new-fallen snow
Gave the lustre of mid-day to objects below,
When, what to my wondering eyes should appear,
But a miniature sleigh, and eight tiny reindeer,
With a little old driver, so lively and quick,
I knew in a moment it must be St. Nick.
More rapid than eagles his coursers they came,
And he whistled, and shouted, and called them by name;
"Now, Dasher! now, Dancer! now, Prancer and Vixen!
On, Comet! on, Cupid! on, Donder and Blitzen!

To the top of the porch! to the top of the wall!
Now dash away! dash away! dash away all!"
As dry leaves that before the wild hurricane fly,
When they meet with an obstacle, mount to the sky;
So up to the house-top the coursers they flew,
With the sleigh full of Toys, and St. Nicholas too.
And then, in a twinkling, I heard on the roof
The prancing and pawing of each little hoof.
As I drew in my head, and was turning around,
Down the chimney St. Nicholas came with a bound.
He was dressed all in fur, from his head to his foot,
And his clothes were all tarnished with ashes and soot;
A bundle of Toys he had flung on his back,
And he looked like a pedler just opening his pack.
His eyes—how they twinkled! his dimples how merry!
His cheeks were like roses, his nose like a cherry!
His droll little mouth was drawn up like a bow
And the beard of his chin was as white as the snow;
The stump of a pipe he held tight in his teeth,
And the smoke it encircled his head like a wreath;
He had a broad face and a little round belly,
That shook when he laughed, like a bowlful of jelly.
He was chubby and plump, a right jolly old elf,
And I laughed when I saw him, in spite of myself;
A wink of his eye and a twist of his head,
Soon gave me to know I had nothing to dread;
He spoke not a word, but went straight to his work,

And filled all the stockings; then turned with a jerk,
And laying his finger aside of his nose,
And giving a nod, up the chimney he rose;
He sprang to his sleigh, to his team gave a whistle,
And away they all flew like the down of a thistle,
But I heard him exclaim, ere he drove out of sight,
"Happy Christmas to all, and to all a good-night."